Because She

Because She Never Asked

•

ENRIQUE VILA-MATAS

Translated by Valerie Miles

A NEW DIRECTIONS PEARL

Manufactured in the United States of America
New Directions Books are printed on acid-free paper
First published as a Pearl (NDP1337) by New Directions in 2015
Design by Erik Rieselbach

Library of Congress Cataloging-in-Publication Data
Vila-Matas, Enrique, 1948–
[Porque ella no lo pidio. English]
Because she never asked / Enrique Vila-Matas ; translated from the Spanish by Valerie Miles. -- First American paperback edition.
pages cm
Translation of a story that appeared in the Enrique Vila-Matas collection Exploradores del abismo, published in Barcelona by Editorial Anagrama in 2007.
ISBN 978-0-8112-2275-4 (alk. paper)
1. Older authors—Fiction. 2. Women artists—Fiction. 3. Reality—Fiction.
4. Meaning (Psychology)—Fiction. 5. Psychological fiction. I. Miles, Valerie, 1963– translator. II. Title.
PQ6672.I37P6713 2015
863'.64—dc23   2015022707

10 9 8 7 6 5 4 3 2 1

New Directions Books are published for James Laughlin
by New Directions Publishing Corporation
80 Eighth Avenue, New York 10011

BECAUSE SHE NEVER ASKED

I. THE JOURNEY OF RITA MALÚ

1

Nobody imitated Sophie Calle better than Rita Malú. Rita liked being considered an artist, though she wasn't entirely sure she was one. Rita carried out a series of experiments with truth, which someone had baptized as *wall novels*; they stood as modest tributes to her beloved Sophie Calle, that "narrative artist" par excellence, who was so close to her in age that only a year separated them. The physical resemblance between the two women was remarkable. If Rita applied her makeup carefully, their faces could be nearly identical, although they were the least alike in height. Rita Malú was a couple inches taller than Sophie Calle (it amused her to tell her friends that Sophie was "tall and worldly," and she was just tall, not at all worldly). If only she were a little shorter, she would be the spitting image of Sophie Calle, who truly was, by the way, a world figure. So Rita's height did represent a bump in the road to an almost absolute likeness. No one could dare say, though, that Rita Malú didn't try to imitate her beloved Sophie Calle in every possible way. For instance, she styled her hair and clothes after Sophie Calle, and she moved to the Malakoff quarter of Paris to be closer to her, where she secretly spied on this woman whose every detail she copied so carefully. Being in the same neighborhood, she was able to keep better tabs on her.

Rita paid careful attention to even the slightest of Sophie Calle's physical fluctuations. She knew where she bought her clothes and food, and every once in a while, she'd follow her into the subway, or trail along behind her in a cab, identifying the people Sophie met outside the Malakoff quarter to know what lovers, friends both male or female, husband, or family she had. Rita dreamed of the day when Sophie Calle would finally realize that she existed and do her the honor of attending one of her exhibitions, held every now and then at an art gallery on Rue de Marseille, a space just below the second-floor apartment where Rita was born.

Despite her move to the Malakoff quarter and the fact that she had a rather hermetic (or perhaps simply melancholic) temperament, Rita was esteemed on Rue de Marseille, and every once in a while the gallery showed her *wall novels*, a peculiar genre of art copied from Sophie Calle: real-life narratives of a novelistic bent told through images centered on the photographer herself and hung on gallery walls.

Rita's relationship with men had always been strange and disconcerting. Her father, a secret millionaire of Mexican origin, died when she was twenty years old and left her a small fortune. Neither she nor anyone else had known he was salting money away for his only daughter. Everyone on Rue de Marseille imagined that soon she'd find herself a boyfriend. She was an attractive girl, after all, if slightly lumbering. She seemed a little uncomfortable in her body, considering herself overly tall, especially when compared with Sophie Calle. As a result, she tended to slouch, trying to adjust her height to something closer to that of her beloved artist. Slouching was a silly thing to do though, and in fact eventually it became detrimental. Honestly, how ridiculous to create such a problem out of being tall.

Rita could be seen talking to the young people in the neighborhood, slouching something dreadful, but she began receding further into herself and her once-secret (now conspicuous) adoration of Sophie Calle. The whole neighborhood loved Rita, and she loved the whole neighborhood and no one in particular. Yet slowly but surely, she grew more aloof and ever more quiet. She overcame her reticence only on certain occasions when she was at home alone or with some suitor. Then she'd whisper in a slightly urbane, well-mannered fashion: "What a bore," before returning to her melancholy state.

The day Rita turned thirty rolled around almost without her noticing, and she realized that she had become the best Sophie Calle imitator in the world. Her devotion had started early on. One day, completely by coincidence, she had come across the first newspaper article ever to mention Sophie Calle. She was immediately enthralled, certainly more than anyone else was. She took note of how much they resembled each other and was captivated by the strange work of this artist who had been born in Paris, just like her, and Rita made up her mind right then and there to begin imitating her, and perhaps in this humble way, to also fill the void in her own life.

By the time she turned thirty-five, Rita had secretly become the very picture of Sophie Calle. Rita hadn't found a boyfriend, and had rejected all her suitors. The day she turned forty, she could be seen in her living room next to a large bouquet of flowers. "Look," she said with an expression of utter chagrin, "I still have suitors." A few months later, she moved out of her place on Rue de Marseille, returning only to exhibit her *wall novels*. She had three more shows, and the last was a series of photographs telling the story of a woman holding a camera and trailing a series of strangers, unnoticed by them. Turning down one suitor after another, Rita could be heard saying, "What a bore," over and over again.

2

One day, Rita Malú decided to ring in the New Year 2006 with a few touch-ups to her life. Not because it was the beginning of the year (when people usually make grand resolutions to change their lives completely), but because she simply couldn't go on, no, she just couldn't bear it any longer; over the past few months she'd become so bored of her home in the Malakoff quarter that she was starting to hate it.

"I hate this domicile," she wrote that morning in red letters in the notebook where she jotted down her moods. The very word *domicile* seemed horrific to her. The first thing she did to change her life was to become a private detective and decorate part of her home to look exactly like Sam Spade's office in *The Maltese Falcon*. Working from movie stills, a few men spent a couple of days installing a glass door like the one in Huston's film, but with Rita's name etched on it instead of Sam Spade's. She arranged the rest of the office on her own, positioning cluttered papers and files just so; she even bought a fan that was utterly useless for that time of year. Next, she placed a classified ad in all the city newspapers: "We can find the most carefully hidden person on the planet. Rita Spade. Private Investigator."

The ad with the office phone number ran for two weeks, but no one called. Nobody requested her services. Eventually, she got sick of waiting around, and thought that if nothing showed up, at least she could use the material for a new Rue de Marseille *wall novel*. She decided to take action. She combed her hair back with pomade, dressed up like a man with a gold-toothed grin, and took four passport photos. She proceeded to show them around in a variety of bars and hotels along Montparnasse, asking if anyone had seen this man in the vicinity, asking questions, really, about her own self.

"Ever seen this guy?" she asked.

No one knew a thing about him. They cracked a few jokes. "Must be a real son of a bitch," they told her at the Select. She'd pull out a card with her office address and telephone number before taking off and ask them to call her if they saw the lug hanging around. "What was his crime?" one of the waiters at the Blue asked. Rita shrugged her shoulders, saying, "Don't know, all I know is that I was hired to look for him." "Think you'll find him?" the waiter asked. Rita made things up as she went along: "I think it'll be easy. I'll find him at home." She sped off, back to the hated domicile, as soon as she saw that the waiter was suitably confused. The day had been worth it after all, if only for the moronic look on that man's face.

3

The phone rang one day, when she least expected it. A woman told Rita Malú that she had a proposition to make, but that she couldn't talk over the phone. At last, a client! Life took on a whole new meaning. They arranged to meet at the dick's office in two hours. The woman, who was very thin, almost thirty, and soberly dressed, had a pale, sad face: her name was Dora. The ad caught her eye, she said—"so original," she emphasized, because it advertised Rita's knack for finding someone in hiding. It fit the profile of the investigator she required. She needed Rita to find the whereabouts of her ex-husband, a famous young writer. He'd been at an undisclosed location for months and had failed to send her the hefty alimony checks he owed her. The writer had published his fifth novel not long ago, in which he staged his own disappearance. And he had now, as it were, vanished into the very text itself. He hadn't been seen since the book was released. Dora had heard rumors that he found haven on Pico Island in the Azores. Lost in the middle of the Atlantic Ocean, the island was basically one colossal volcano. Dora's ex-husband had already written about the island in one of his earlier novels, so he was very familiar with the place, and surely that's where he was hiding out, but it was too remote for her to track him down herself. She was sure that the agency—she would pay spectacularly well—could investigate and discover his whereabouts, whether on Pico Island or anywhere else. "Just find him," she said, "and get him to do me the goddamn favor of paying the alimony."

It took Rita Malú all of five minutes to be rid of any doubt about what was going on. The missing writer did exist, his name was Jean Turner, Rita had heard about him once. Up to that point everything made sense. But clearly this first client of hers, this woman, was batty. Dora must have read one of Turner's books, fallen in love with it, and as a result, she now alleged and wanted to believe that the main character of the book (the young writer) was her ex-husband.

Rita felt a pang of fear when she realized she was dealing with a very unstable individual. It took a considerable effort to finally get rid of the client, and she swore to dismantle the office the very next day. Game over. This road could only lead to more deranged clients. She went to bed and dreamt about a little red house, a house she adored, atop a small promontory. Unable to resist its spell, she knocked at the door of the little house until finally an old man answered. Just as she opened her mouth to tell him something, she woke up. But the red house persisted in her memory for days to come; both the house and the old man. Maybe, she thought, they really exist somewhere.

The visit of the strange, lunatic client had unsettled her for some reason. So the next day she went out and bought the novel by this young writer, this Jean Turner, whom that poor woman thought was her ex-husband. The back-cover copy established that Turner did indeed narrate his own disappearance in the book, but hours later Rita would also discover that the author had only disappeared in the pages of the book. In real life, he'd simply retired to Pico Island and hadn't tried to hide the fact from anyone.

What to make of it all? Rita stared at Turner's photo on the back cover: a young man of thirty, very tall, extremely thin, with bat ears, a narrow face, and a bushy chestnut-colored beard; he wore a moth-eaten coat, a baseball cap, and a navy-blue scarf. He was rather unpleasant looking. But she had bought the book and his four earlier ones, too. After all, and without even realizing it, she had been relieved by poor Turner of the boredom of her daily life. Later that same afternoon, she came across repeated references of the Azores in his fourth book, where he mentioned Peter's Bar a number of times, in the town of Horta on Faial Island, the one just beside Pico.

Rita stuck to her decision to shut down the sterile detective office and forego her less-than-exciting rounds of Montparnasse bars, where she'd been asking questions about her own self. It now occurred to her that it was time to travel. Why not escape the monotony? Why not travel to the Azores to find a man like, say, Turner? She'd never pursued a man before. And a natural outcome of never having pursued a man could be traveling to the Azores to find a vulgar, ugly fellow of no concern to her whatsoever. The man was insignificant, this writer with a bushy, chestnut-colored beard. Why not spend some time, perhaps begin an adventure like Lewis Carroll's Alice (whom she'd so loved in adolescence), and wander around aimlessly to and fro, not worrying about whatever took her from one place to another?

4

Rita arrived in Lisbon three days later, ready to skip over to the Azores. She carried a small, abridged version of Sophie Calle's work in her suitcase (a sort of Marcel Duchampian *boite-en-valise*), along with a book by Simone Weil. Rita had been disconcerted by Weil's contempt for the imaginative arts, which Weil considered mere tricks to camouflage the immense void of our mortality.

She decided to see a bit of Lisbon first and postpone her connecting flight to Faial Island in the Azores until the next day. The day was cold, almost wintry. And Rita, without quite knowing why—almost as if she were receiving some kind of command, as if someone behind her, thinking she wasn't going anywhere, had ordered her to go somewhere—journeyed to that frightening place near Lisbon, Boca do Inferno. Only three kilometers from Cascais, it's a ghastly spot in the winter. The tide comes in hard, filling the coves and rock crevices, howling dreadfully, and blowing crests of spray high on stormy days.

Boca do Inferno is the spot where the people of Lisbon traditionally commit suicide. Oddly, or at least contrary to the habitual practice of asking God for traveling mercies, Rita commended herself to the ghost of the magician and Satanist Aleister Crowley, who traveled to Lisbon in 1930 to meet Fernando Pessoa. He faked his own disappearance at Boca do Inferno, leaving a suicide note in his gold cigarette case. The message spread across the globe, since the Satanist was a very famous man, and also because his accomplice took it upon himself to notify Lisbon's *Diário de Notícias*.

At Boca do Inferno, Rita imitated the diabolical Crowley and left her own note in a cigarette case she'd bought on Rua dos Douradores, announcing her suicide to the world and taking leave of Sophie Calle with words of love, written in Portuguese.

A few minutes later, unexpectedly, she felt as though, for this rather gratuitous act of writing the note, she was being thanked for being such a good sport; she was being rewarded by being taken spiritually very far, away from herself. And what was even stranger: she had the impression, for what seemed the eternity of a few seconds, that she had actually turned into the real Sophie Calle.

She felt herself shrinking a few centimeters.

So she wrote another suicide note, substituting it for the previous one in the cigarette case. The message said exactly the same thing. (*Nao posso viver sem ti. A outra Boca do Inferno apañar-me-á—nao sera tao quente como a tua*; I cannot live without you. The other Boca do Infierno will receive me— it will not be as hot as yours!) Only this time it was signed by Sophie Calle.

Then she snapped to and left Boca do Inferno, slouching visibly, as if her suitcase weighed heavily. There is a goal but no path: what we call a path is but a series of hesitations, she thought, in order just to think.

5

Two days later, Rita Malú arrived on Faial, the island next to Pico, her resolve strengthened by the fact that she had never pursued a man before and by her idea that what she was doing was merely a variation on the theme of not pursuing someone. In other words, she was traveling to the Azores to find some ugly, vulgar fellow who was really of no concern to her anyway.

Out in the middle of the Atlantic, a long distance from everything, both Europe and America, the islands seemed, at first, the very essence of "far away." Distance was part of their allure, perhaps. In any case, the place was ideal for being far from the madding crowd. Her first sunset there was indolent and very slow. A beautiful, bloody twilight. She scrutinized it from the balcony of her room at the Hostal Santa Cruz on Faial, looking out at mysterious Pico Island in front of her.

Pico Island is a volcanic cone that juts abruptly out of the ocean; a precipitous mountain perched atop the sea. No more than three small coastal towns nestle along the foot of the mountain: Madalena, Sao Roque, and Lajes, the latter with its small whaling museum. Contemplating the volcano's hazy silhouette surreptitiously from Faial was all it took for her to get a sense of the island's strange and disturbing nature. And it was even stranger in the wintertime, as now. The closer one got to the island, the more it commanded respect, as if one were being called to the very gates of things past.

Café Sport on Faial Island, also known as Peter's Bar, was an extraordinary place: something between a tavern, a meeting hall, an information bureau, and a post office. The old whalers hung out there, as did people from ships on their way across the Atlantic or on other long-distance journeys. There was a wood-framed bulletin board with all sorts of notes stuck to it: telegrams, letters, made-up memories, drawings of boats inscribed with sentences by people who seemed shipwrecked from their own lives.

The mythical figure, José Azevedo, whom the English baptized with the nickname Peter during World War II, had died a few weeks before Rita Malú arrived at Café Sport. Now his son José Henrique Azevedo ran the bar that was founded a century earlier to serve drinks to foreigners, the Atlantic's lonesome sailors, and the whalers. The weather along the channel between Pico and Faial Islands was stormy, so the ferries weren't running that day. Rita wasn't in any hurry to get to Pico and find the writer with the bushy chestnut beard. What could she possibly say to the man when she located him? She probably wouldn't dare say anything at all.

So she spent two full days waiting for the weather to settle, conversing with the old whalers at Café Sport, taking their photos as they told passionate tales of the days when hunting cetaceans was permitted in the Azores.

In *Moby-Dick*, Herman Melville wrote that the bravest whalers in the world came from the Azores. With that in mind, Rita left the bar each day feeling closer to the heirs of those titans, men who told her old sea tales, which she jotted down in her notebook. Registering these stories about the ancient whalers' lost world made her feel as though she were living happy moments in her life; perhaps this was the closest she'd ever felt—more even than at Boca do Inferno—to Sophie Calle, that person she always discreetly imitated.

At night, carefully writing out some of the yarns she had recorded during the day, she would imagine the show she'd put together at Rue de Marseille when she got back to Paris, she might even dare to invite Sophie Calle, to show her how her most devoted copycat was now able to impersonate her so truly. Rita would create a staggering *wall novel* with all these old whalers on Faial. The entire neighborhood would see what she was capable of.

She felt nearly perfect. After all, she was hearing more than just whale-hunting tales. She'd also been made privy to spy stories from World War II, when Faial was a strategic spot and a supply point for Allied ships and American seaplanes, the famous clippers that anchored in Horta Bay in front of Café Sport.

Two days after her arrival in Faial, Rita Malú decided to play another one of her private jokes. She hung an anonymous message on Café Sport's bulletin board, careful that nobody saw her do it: "I'm shipwrecked from my own life, here to reject my last suitor." Rita was sure that nobody would suspect her of leaving the note, this ordinary journalist who was just hanging around, worried (although they couldn't possibly imagine as much), that the bad weather in the channel would abate, obliging her to board the Pico Island ferry to find the suitor she must reject; nobody was asking her to do it (really nobody had asked her to do anything), yet she sensed that somehow this rejection would allow her to say goodbye, once and for all, to the ghost of love.

"Love? I believe in it, but it's not for me. I've never been and never will be in love," Rita wrote on a small piece of paper she posted a few hours later, again, when no one was watching, in the spot where the love missives hung on Café Sport's charming wooden bulletin board.

Good weather finally allowed the ferry across to Pico the next day. A few old whalers, now her fastidious suitors, had offered to escort her, but Rita found a way to avoid the companionship of so many impertinent men. She pulled a wedding photo out of her luggage to get them to back off, a picture she carried around if she ever needed to shoo any horseflies away. It was really another woman: Sophie Calle playing the part of a bride at her false wedding, though it was hard to tell the difference. Everyone took it to be Rita on her wedding day, since she looked so much like the artist she impersonated.

"What a bore," she said, taking leave of the men as she boarded the ferry that was heading for Pico Island and its spectacular volcano, the tallest mountain in Portugal. Very few people were on board, she counted eight in all, each one carrying a wicker basket or woven bag; there wasn't a single tourist among them. Rita was gripped by a sense of estrangement that intensified the closer she got to the island. Luckily, she knew what she had to do when she got there. She had read in an episode of Jean Turner's penultimate novel that there were two cab drivers on the island: a young one and an old one. She knew not to waste a second over determining which one to hire; it had to be the older one, since the younger driver, according to Turner, was reckless. Which is exactly what she did when she landed on Pico Island. She hadn't bothered to look up the writer's address from Faial, in fact, she hadn't even pronounced his name once the entire trip. All she had to do was ask the older cab driver to take her to the town of Lajes, just like one of the characters in Turner's novel. And just like that character, she would also say she wanted to visit the Whaling Museum. And she would wait until she was in the cab before asking the whereabouts of this tall, thin young man with the bushy beard, in whose world of fictitious reality she had been circulating for some days now.

The port village of Madalena was like a ghost town. The eight people disembarked from the ferry and disappeared within a few seconds of landing, vanishing into the town's tiny labyrinth of streets. The town was deserted at that time of year, or at least during these hours of the day. And there they were, two taxis waiting for the ferry to arrive. It seemed as if they had already been notified of Rita's presence on board from the port in Faial. She walked straight to the older cab driver, got into his car, and asked him to take her to the Whaling Museum in Lajes. The younger driver cursed, acting as though he had expected this to happen all along; perhaps the curses were insults also meant for Turner.

The road connecting Madalena with Lajes skirted the base of the volcano, a curvy, narrow route full of deep potholes that ran along a breakwater or seawall and looked out over a deep-blue, rebellious Atlantic. The road crossed through land that had once been covered in vineyards and the sumptuous houses of patricians (all fallen to ruin); now the land was rocky and melancholic, dotted with strange, solitary, minimalist houses scattered atop low, windswept hills.

Rita figured the time had come to inquire after Turner and asked the driver if he could take her to the house where the island's writer lived. The driver didn't understand Rita's Portuguese very well and thought she was asking about a writing desk. "No store in Pico sells such things," he said. This is exactly what happened in the novel of the writer she was looking for, and Rita couldn't help but think how funny it was, how sublime even, this impression of living out what's in the pages of a book, a book that had already been written.

As expected—they had already told her as much on Faial—the Whaling Museum in Lajes was closed. So her search for the hidden author was nearing its end. "What a bore," she sighed, whispering to herself that Turner, too, was like a closed museum. A shipwreck of her own life, Rita Malú wanted to return to Peter's Bar, where she had enjoyed impersonating Sophie Calle without anyone being the wiser. As far as Turner was concerned, she preferred not to see him. What for?

Before returning to the pier at Madalena, Rita decided to visit the church in Lajes and walk around for a while. Later, she invited the cab driver for a coffee in the town square, where he recounted the splendors of his youth on Pico Island, in a tone filled with melancholy. "Men are so boring," she murmured. A little while later, they headed back to the pier.

As they drew nearer to Madalena, they came to a bend in the road. Rita spied a short trail leading to a small red house that was identical to the one in her dream a few days earlier. She asked the driver to stop and wasn't surprised to see how the path wound briefly up to the small top of a tree-covered hill, exactly as in her dream. It came to rest in front of the red house, whose tiniest details she now remembered with sharp precision.

It felt as though she had always been there, ever since her dream about this house whose door had been opened to her by an old man. The closer she got to this tiny red house, the more she felt compelled to knock at its door, pulled by its peculiar attraction. So she did exactly that, she knocked. The old man from her dream opened the door to her once again, only this time he was a towering and extremely thin old man with bat ears, a narrow face, and a bushy white beard. His coat was moth-eaten. It was Turner all right, but fifty years older. Unlike in her dream, Rita was now able to talk to the old man, and it occurred to her to ask if the house was for sale. It was, but the old man cautioned her against buying it.

"A ghost haunts this house," the old man explained.

There was a brief silence.

"What ghost?" she asked.

"You," the old man said, and he softly closed the door.

II. DON'T MESS WITH ME

1

I wrote the story "The Journey of Rita Malú" for Sophie Calle. You could say I did it because she asked me to. It all began one afternoon when she called me at my home in Barcelona. I was flabbergasted. I revered her and considered her out of reach. I'd never met her in person and didn't think I ever would. She had called to say that a mutual friend (Isabel Coixet) had given her my phone number, and that she wanted to propose something, but couldn't do it over the phone.

Her words carried a strange, mysterious charge to them, however much she didn't intend them to be that way. I suggested an encounter in Paris at the end of the month since I planned on spending New Year's Eve there; 2005 was drawing to a close. We arranged to meet at the Café de Flore in Paris at noon on the 27th of December.

On the appointed day, I arrived in the neighborhood a half hour early, a little anxious over our encounter. Sophie Calle had something of a reputation for being capable of practically anything, and I was well aware of her eccentricities and audacity, partly thanks to Paul Auster's novel

Leviathan, in which Sophie is a character named Maria Turner. Auster's dedication at the beginning reads: "The author extends special thanks to Sophie Calle for permission to mingle fact with fiction."

I was already aware of all this, but I knew a lot of other things, too. For example, I recalled reading how once, when Sophie was young, she had felt lost in her home city of Paris after returning from a long trip through Lebanon. She wasn't familiar with anyone anymore and felt compelled to follow people she had never met, so they would decide where she was supposed to go. I recalled this and some of her other famous "actions": how she invited strangers to sleep in her bed as long as they let her observe and photograph them and answered her questions (*The Sleepers*); or how she had pursued a man one time after she found out purely by chance that he was traveling to Venice that evening (*Venetian Suite*); or how she got her mother to hire a private detective to follow her around and take photographs of her (knowing the whole time that she was being trailed) to have him profile her in his reports with the fake, naked truth of an objective observer.

On the way to our appointment at the Café de Flore, I was reminded of what Vicente Molina Foix had said about Sophie Calle, how she belonged to the realm of the verbal imagination. Considering the models that inspired her and the fact that words were always at the origin of her visual projects, considering her earnest personal accounts and the strong prose she used to tell the stories in which she established herself as the protagonist—victim and subject of an omniscient narration—Sophie Calle stood as one of the greatest novelists of our time.

I came to the appointment feeling uneasy, and asked myself what she could possibly have in store for me, if it might be something bizarre or dangerous. To buck up my self-confidence before our meeting, I ducked into the nearby Café Bonaparte and threw back two shots of whisky in less than five minutes, standing at the bar Wild West style. I left Café Bonaparte walking slowly (it was ten minutes to twelve) and stopped to have a look in the window of La Hune bookstore, which is only ten meters away from the Flore. The French translation of one of my novels was on display, but I didn't pay much attention to it; I was too busy questioning myself about what Sophie Calle was going to say.

Suddenly, a little man with North African features asked very politely if I had a minute to talk. I thought he was going to ask for money and was irritated that he had pulled my concentration away from Sophie Calle.

"Pardon me, but I've been observing you and would like to offer my help," the man said. He handed me the address for Alcoholics Anonymous, written on a piece of paper that was torn from a small notebook. He had been following me since the Bonaparte. I didn't know how to respond. I considered telling him that I wasn't an alcoholic, or anonymous. I thought of explaining to him that I didn't drink as much as might appear and also that I wasn't exactly an anonymous person, and then drawing his attention to my book on display in the window. But I didn't say a word. I pocketed the address and tried to walk into the Flore without slouching or seeming complex-ridden.

I recognized Sophie Calle immediately from among the others. She had arrived early and got a table in a good spot. I asked her permission to sit down in a show of respect. She smiled and extended it, explaining that we would speak in Spanish, she had lived in Mexico for a year and knew my language well. I sat down, curbing my shyness by starting to talk immediately. I told her the story about how I had been spied on and pursued just a moment before by a recovering alcoholic; both the man and the chase seemed like something straight out of one of the *wall novels* Sophie was so addicted to. Might she have been responsible for putting him up to it?

Sophie smiled slightly and almost without further ado pointed out an excerpt from my most popular novel. The excerpt, she said, related directly to what she wanted to propose. I could hardly recall that particular episode in my book. It recounted a story that Marcel Schwob tells in *Parallel Lives*: one about the life of Petronius, who when he turned thirty, it's said, decided to narrate his forays into the seamy side of the city. He wrote sixteen books of his own invention and when he had finished, read them aloud to Sirius, his accomplice and slave, who laughed like a lunatic and applauded ceaselessly. So the two together, Sirius and Petronius, came up with the scheme of living out the adventures he had written, taking them from parchment to reality. Petronius and Sirius dressed up in costume and fled the city, taking to the open road and living out the adventures Petronius had composed. Petronius abandoned writing from that moment on, once he began living the life he had imagined. "In other words," I ended saying in the excerpt, "if the theme of *Don Quixote* is about the dreamer who dares to become what he dreams, the story of Petronius is that of the writer who dares to experience what he has written, and for that reason stops writing."

What Sophie suggested was that I write a story, any story. That I create a character she could bring to life: one whose behavior, for a maximum of one year's time, would be contingent upon what I wrote. She wanted to change her life and what's more, she was tired of having to determine her own *deeds*; now she preferred to have someone else do it for her, to allow somebody else to decide how she was supposed to live. She would obey the *author* in everything. There was a brief silence. Everything, that is, except killing, she said.

"In short, you write a story, and I'll bring it to life."

2

We remained silent for a few long seconds, till she regained her voice and explained to me that she had made the same proposition to Paul Auster some years earlier, but he had considered it too great a responsibility and declined. She also mentioned her more recent offer to Jean Echenoz, who also ended up declining the invitation.

It seemed to me that the intention behind Sophie's proposition was to make the author disappear, which is precisely what I claimed to desire so much in my latest writing. But I hadn't dared follow through with it, I'd only blurred my personality into the text a bit. Sophie was aware of my concerns, I told myself, and surely that's why she had chosen me now, to bring my literature to life once and for all.

She explained that her mother had only two or three months left to live, it was important for me to keep this in mind; that was the only thing that might temporarily delay our common project, given, of course, that I was willing to accept her proposition.

"I haven't responded yet, but I'm happy to accept," I said.

Sophie smiled. I've always thought that a smile is the perfect form of laughter. She seemed happy that I had hardly doubted a second before accepting. But I shouldn't forget, she reminded me again, that everything depended on the state of her mother's health.

3

Half an hour later, I was back in the Hotel Littré on rue Littré, where my wife was waiting for me. I excitedly explained this strange assignment to her. I was satisfied and even impressed with the prospect that had just opened in my life, although perhaps it would be better to say in my work, since the life bit was Sophie's task. The problem now was figuring out what kind of story to write. At first, all I came up with were stupidities: making Sophie travel to Barcelona, for example, and sign up to take Catalan classes. Truly asinine things like that. My wife suggested that I make more of an effort. "You'll come up with something. You always find a way out when you get stuck," she told me.

I returned to Barcelona with my wife the next day. I figured the sooner I wrote the story, the better. I had a burning curiosity to clarify things as soon as possible; in other words, to find out as soon as I could how things would play out and to calculate whether I was truly interested in being involved in this attractive, though strange and uncertain, project. I worried that if I let too much time go by, Sophie

Calle might back out or maybe even forget her proposition. So I went straight to work as soon as I returned to Barcelona and wrote "The Journey of Rita Malú."

I emailed "The Journey of Rita Malú" to Sophie precisely on January 12. I was confident that she'd try to bring the story to life (and I was eager to see how she would go about it. Would she find the ghost, for example, who was my own self, only fifty years older?). Her answer by return email was slow to arrive. Days went by without a word from her, not a single message. I obliged myself to write something every day in my diary (I had been keeping a sort of diary in a red notebook since September), so I noted that she hadn't yet given any sign of having received my story. Had my story not appealed to her? Could she have figured out that it was really an exploration of mental geographies in pursuit of a ghostly writer, who was in fact my own self, though visibly older?

The lack of a response certainly provoked in me a sense of uncertainty. It wasn't that I thought the work was poorly written. My story was in keeping with what she had requested. What's more, it was an elastic narrative that could either be a complete short story or otherwise the first chapter of a novel. So it offered a level of freedom: to climb aboard the story and live it out as a complete novel, or settle into the piece merely as a first chapter, a short story, and then step off early in the journey.

The days went by with no news from Sophie, until one afternoon I realized that her strange silence was crippling me as a writer. For the first time in my life, I was depending on someone else to be able to write: I needed this other person to move into action, I mean she had to start living out what I wrote and then ask me to continue the story if the occasion called for it. Obviously, what I couldn't do now (which is what I was accustomed to doing when I wrote novels) was continue writing about the ghost of the Azores on my own; I couldn't write anything else until she acted on the story, discovered the ghost, and asked what happened next, if in fact she wanted to follow the story onward.

Sophie's silence made me anxious. What's more, her lack of an answer left me vulnerable, literally paralyzed and incapable of writing. I was poised for a new book that couldn't go anywhere because it wasn't in my hands to make it happen. I began to wonder whether one of the intentions behind Sophie Calle's project wasn't to do me in as a writer.

4

I had warned Sophie when we met at the Flore that I would be traveling on January 23 to a literary conference in Cartagena de Indias, Colombia. She seemed to make a mental note of the information, because when her long overdue answer finally arrived, it came on the very 23rd of January (eleven days after I sent my story to her), precisely and peculiarly on the same day I left Barcelona for Colombia. My wife, worried over how uneasy I'd become over the whole affair, called my hotel in Cartagena to let me know that Sophie Calle had finally responded and that the email went like this: "I haven't received anything from you yet, although no rush. I've had problems with my Internet, broke down last week. I'm afraid you might think (in case you sent me something) that I've been keeping silent."

I realized we'd practically have to start all over. So upon my return from Cartagena, I resent "The Journey of Rita Malú" to Sophie. And that's when it got worse. Once again, days of a newfound, strange silence passed. My angst expressed itself in troubled notes, written in my diary or red notebook.

Finally, a message from Sophie arrived on February 3rd: "My mother wanted to see the sea one last time before she died and we've traveled to Cabourg. As to what concerns us, I finally found out why I never received your emails or your story: it all went into my spam box, including poor Rita Malú. I will begin to read your story very soon."

I remember dreaming that night that Cabourg was the capital of one of the Azore Islands. But the dream was much calmer than the previous ones. As if Sophie's promise to read my story had a soothing effect on me.

5

Remember to distrust.
—Stendhal

The next day I went to Girona to present at a conference. Later, I had dinner with some friends, where I outlined a few details of the project I had gotten involved in with Sophie Calle. I had been drinking, and the alcohol had put me on edge. I felt the need to explain everything to them, as if I were writing by proxy, since I couldn't do it for real. I had to cross my arms and wait for Sophie to decide to make a move. Naturally, I could begin a story or a novel that had nothing to do with Sophie's scheme, but I was incapable of setting off on a parallel venture.

"I'm paralyzed," I told them, "because I can't wish for the death of Sophie's mother in order to resume work on my novel. I can't do anything, I can't even write her an email. Nor can I show polite interest in her mother's health, since it might seem as though I wished for something critical to happen to her that would allow me to get back to working on the project."

I ended by invoking the pathetic case of Truman Capote in *In Cold Blood*: the writer who suffered unspeakably from not being able to finish the book without the execution scene.

When I got back from Girona, I couldn't stand the inactivity any longer and was overcome by a suicidal urge to press the send key and shoot over to Sophie a beautiful image of the volcanic Island of Pico, which looked vaguely reminiscent of Roberto Rosellini's movie *Stromboli*. Something had to happen, anything, if only a slight breeze, I remember saying to myself.

She answered with surprising briskness that same day. The picture she sent frightened me, because it was her elderly mother's face with a severe look in her eyes, as if she were reproaching my obscene impatience to see her dead. Sophie had written below the photo: "I'm sending a picture of my mother. It's the one she picked to decorate her grave, and the epitaph will read: *I was getting bored*. I'm sending it to you because in a way she's what's standing between me and Pico Island. I've heard that you'll be in Paris on the 16th of March. Perhaps we could see each other then."

In fact, I did have to be at the Salon du Livre in Paris on the 16th of March. But the date was so far away. It seemed way too long to have to wait for another encounter. It seemed to me as if the two of us were doomed to communicate in fits and starts. But what else could I do? The lack of action had me feeling restless, but I couldn't very well murder Sophie's mother in order for Sophie to kick into gear and get started with the journey.

In my red notebook, I jotted: "Someone in Paris wants me to reveal the fact that I no longer want to write. And she's going about it in infinitely perverse ways. I must write about it in order to continue writing."

A few days later, I dared myself to send Sophie a new email that might break this deadlock, though I tried not to get my hopes up. I wrote:

"All life is a process of breaking down" (Francis Scott Fitzgerald).

I pressed the send key. There was no way back now. It was irreversible. The sentence about breaking down had already traveled to Sophie's inbox. Minutes later, again with surprising speed, Sophie answered with the photo of a grave that read *Don't expect anything*.

I took it very hard. As if that *Don't expect anything* was meant for me. I responded immediately, desperate to defend my self-respect. I sent her a quote by Julien Gracq that went: "The writer has nothing to expect from others. Believe me, he writes only for himself!"

Once again, silence fell over our correspondence. A silence that reigned for days. One afternoon at the end of February, I ran into my friend Sergi Pàmies and vented my frustration by conveying the whole story of Sophie Calle and the strange labyrinth of emails in which I had gotten lost. To keep him interested, I absurdly reminded him that just like Sophie, he had been born in Paris. Obviously, there was no need to dwell on such a thing. Sergi listened to me with his customary kindness and curiosity, and after thinking it over a while, insinuated something rather dreadful, something that had already occurred to me, too. He said that perhaps Sophie's mother wasn't on her last legs after all, and the point of the game was in the exchange of emails, which Sophie Calle would turn into a *wall novel,* a study of my ethical behavior during the silent wait for the supposed death of her mother.

"You might just find all the emails you've been writing to Sophie reproduced someday in large format on the walls of some museum," Pàmies told me. "Be careful what you write from now on, because you might be reading it through a magnifying glass in the near future."

When I described how the relationship between Sophie and me had taken on the structure of a love story (the jealousy of one person not knowing what the other was thinking, which is really what lover's jealousy has always been about: not knowing what the other is thinking; read Proust to understand it better), Sergi preferred not to wax transcendent and instead mentioned a French song called "Les histoires d'amour," sung by the Rita Mitsouko Duo. "Love stories generally end badly," Rita Mitsouko sang.

6

When I got home later that day, I was surprised to find Sophie's response to my Julien Gracq quote. This time there was no text, only the tiny photograph of a funerary cross. Irritated by the mute and solitary cross, I decided to banish the image by resending it to Sergi, who had just emailed me the full text of the song by the Rita Mitsouko Duo.

"Sergi, look what that Sophie sent me," I wrote. But oh, horror of horrors, I hadn't been paying enough attention and in my haste, I actually resent the message to Sophie herself. It wouldn't be long before she found out that I had referred to her somewhat disrespectfully as "that Sophie," and, what's worse, that I was forwarding her emails to someone named Sergi.

As soon as I realized my mistake, I was mortified.

The days went by in ominous, strict, horrendous silence. Surely, it was all over.

One afternoon, suddenly, when I least expected it, an email arrived: "I hope you didn't think my *plurien* meant anything."

Did this *plurien* refer to her *Don't expect anything*? Her sentence came accompanied by the image of a road leading into a town called Faux. I understood there was clearly a message here for me: she was calling me a "fake." And even more obvious, or what seemed to be finally confirmed: it was over between us; I had proved that I was a pig.

7

I spent several days in a daze, writing down small, ridiculous notes in my red notebook. Crushed. Until one morning, carried away by the alcohol-infused bliss of the previous night, I began telling myself that I had nothing to lose by trying to reconcile with Sophie, so I dared send her an email: "I will be in Paris from the 16th to the 21st of March, at the Hotel de Suède, on Rue Vaneau. Since they don't always inform their guests of missed telephone calls, I wanted to advise that if you'd like to reach me, it would be best to communicate by fax."

My real motive, should Sophie decide to answer, was to see whether a fax would be admitted into the collection of emails that were probably en route to becoming one of her hypothetical *wall novels*. I sent the message, and, as my mother said when my father went off to do the lengthy military service required in their day, bracing for the duration with no idea when he would be coming home, *I sat down to wait.* That's just what I did over the following days: I sat down to wait, nesting at my desk at all hours without writing a thing, nothing more than waiting and thinking,

thinking about a variety of subjects. I ruminated. I calculated, for example, how long it would take for spring to arrive and I remember telling myself things like: With the arrival of spring, one must be ironic; and I know that only by so being, I will survive the next season. Things like that, sometimes without much sense. Until the 16th of March came around, and off I went to the Hotel de Suède on Rue Vaneau, in Paris.

I had only been at the hotel a few hours when a fax from Sophie arrived, encouraging me to call her at home. My first reaction was a combination of happiness and annoyance. On the one hand, there was nothing I wanted more than her forgiveness, but, on the other, I thought of how aggravating the rebirth of this complicated relationship might be.

After much hesitation, I finally made up my mind to call her. The telephone rang three times. Someone picked up.

"It's me … I'm …," I babbled.

A brief silence. Followed by Sophie's voice:

"Oh! You got my fax?"

"Yes, I'm here in Paris. Is everything well, Sophie?"

Another brief silence. And then she whispered these words:

"My mother died yesterday afternoon."

It's the last thing I expected to hear. I didn't know whether to believe her or not. It seemed too much of a coincidence that her mother should wait until I got to Paris to die. I was at a loss. Finally, I mumbled a few words of condolence.

"Oh, come on," she interrupted.

Another phone rang in Sophie's house, probably her cell phone, and she asked me to "excuse her for a second." I heard part of her conversation with the person who had called. She pronounced the word "funeral" several times, and it made me think that however unlikely it seemed, the truth about the death of her mother (which seemed like a beastly farce) was actually confirmed.

She hung up her cell phone and came back to our conversation, telling me the funeral would take place two days later in the cemetery of Montparnasse, and that it would be nice if I could come. The obituary would appear in *Liberation* on the day of the funeral. In any case, she added, now she had the time to see me. If I wanted, we could meet somewhere in Paris within the hour. In the Hotel de Suède, for example.

An hour and five minutes later, Sophie walked into the hall of the Hotel de Suède with a video camera and a broad smile. I was in the hall waiting for her. She ordered two coffees in reception, and although I didn't want to see them, she showed me recent pictures of her dead mother and a copy of the peculiar obituary that would appear in *Liberation* two days later.

It didn't take long for her to explain that following the experience with her mother, there was still one more obstacle between her and Pico Island. She had been invited to the Venice Biennale and needed time to prepare her show in this noteworthy exhibition. She was so sorry, but our project would have to be postponed. She had studied maps of the Azores and was also drawn to the idea of returning to Lisbon, a city she wasn't very familiar with after all. It wasn't a lack of interest in Rita Malu's journey, on the contrary, she was very engaged with it, but the Venice Biennale was, as I must perfectly understand, of paramount importance to her.

Of course I understood perfectly, but there was a question hanging in the air that I didn't hesitate to ask:

"When will you have time to live out 'The Journey of Rita Malú?'"

"May of next year," she said, without blinking.

My God! May 2007 seemed so far away. What was I going to do in the meantime?

"I've been waiting a long time, over eight years, to tackle this experience of *living* a story and I don't mind waiting another year," she added by way of explanation.

"Eight years?"

"Yes, eight years have passed since I first proposed the idea to Paul Auster. I can wait a little while longer, don't you think?"

It seemed the perfect occasion to stage a break-up, to convey to her that by no means would I wait fourteen more months; so be it, our imaginary contract had come to an end. No way would I wait such a ridiculous amount of time!

But instead I was all smiles and resignedly docile.

We said our goodbyes at the door of the hotel an hour later and arranged to see each other again the following day, at the Salon du Livre, Porte de Versailles, where I would be signing copies of my latest novel. She would come to see me, she said, since it was near her home. I took my leave, and we both headed to our respective appointments, walking in opposite directions. I went to a friend's party near Bastille Square, where I described a few details of my recent encounter with Sophie. A journalist from a magazine dedicated to rock music and literature heard my story and blurted: "Oh my God! She approached you about it, too?"

I didn't really want to know what she meant by "you, too." But I ended up saying, "Yes, she approached me, too." Then I asked if she had approached anyone other than Paul Auster or Jean Echenoz. And yes, she had suggested the idea to two other writers. And, she had also approached Olivier Rolin.

The next day, I found out that there had been not just three more writers, but at least four. Just before I left Littré for the Salon du Livre, I received a call from a good friend of mine who was in Segovia, the writer and filmmaker Ray Loriga, who invited me to Madrid to participate in *Carta Libre*, an hour-long program on Spanish public television, on which he interviewed artists from his imaginary tribe. He wanted to invite Sophie and me as his guests, to talk about our project, he said. I asked him how he had found out about it, and he told me that Sophie had told him herself, they were longtime friends. She had made the same attractive proposition to him three years

47

ago. He'd almost gone mad, he said, working relentlessly to move the seductive proposal forward; he'd come up against all sorts of peculiar glitches, including Sophie herself. Luckily for him, he hadn't gotten so far as to write the story. My case was definitely much worse, since my story was already written and nothing had come of it.

How aggravating to discover that there had been more people invited to do the project before me, and I'd never been told about them. But I didn't speak out and kept my anger to myself. I accepted Loriga's invitation to his program, figuring that at least it would give me another opportunity to see Sophie, and more material to put into writing about my relationship with her, this holding pattern that was threatening to become eternal, as I awaited her decision to embark on the adventure: Rita Malú's journey toward the encounter with my ghost.

8

Two hours later, I was signing copies of my novel in the Salon du Livre, when Sophie showed up with a friend whom she introduced as Florence Aubenas, that is, the famous journalist of *Liberation,* who had been kidnapped and then freed in Iraq. Though I had signed the petition for her release in Barcelona, I hadn't seen photographs of her. So, inevitably, I doubted that this woman was the real Aubenas. Inertia led me to suspect that everything Sophie did was a bluff; she had lied to me about her mother and now she wanted to poke fun at me by introducing me to the fake Aubenas.

"Stop pulling my leg," I said to Sophie.

It came from the gut. I uttered it spontaneously; it just burst out as a result of all these ambiguities. Now I was getting overly familiar with her.

"What do you mean, stop pulling my leg? Do you mean that you don't want me to play with you?" Sophie asked in very good Spanish.

"Exactly," I smiled. "Don't mess with me."

That seemed to me a good title for a novel.

But Florence Aubenas was in fact Florence Aubenas. Everyone around me confirmed it. Even Aubenas confirmed that she was herself; she invited me to her stand where she signed a copy of her recently published book, *La méprise*. So I went back to mine, to my stand that is, and continued signing books. Every once in a while, Sophie would show up, walking back and forth between Florence's and my publisher's stand.

Sophie would appear and stare straight at me, then laugh in an infectious way. I would end up laughing too, my expression distorted after uselessly trying to keep a straight face, or to express anger.

"Don't mess with me," I told her again.

I giggled. That was it. The next day, I returned to Barcelona, and Sophie attended her mother's funeral. It seemed silly to reproach her for having propositioned so many men to bring a written adventure to life, having so many broken friends. It seemed grotesque to criticize her, and what's more, I had no right whatsoever.

The idea was hers, after all, and she could perform it with whomever she pleased, whenever she pleased. I convinced myself (so as not to lose my wits) that it was all beyond reproach. I had no reason for feeling so apprehensive. Why not wait until May? But ... it was May of next year! I was peeved, annoyed, over having been so submissive the whole time, about our agreeing that I would control what was to be done and what had to be lived out. I couldn't understand why I was being so docile. Anyway,

I thought, I would have another chance to rebel against the situation on my friend Ray Loriga's television show; at least I'd be able to pound the table a little with my fist. I was hostage to the strange sensation of gripping a rock-solid hammer in my hand, but not being able to use it because its handle was in flames.

9

Back in Barcelona, I received an email from Sophie letting me know that she would arrive in Madrid to tape the show on the 6th of April, as long as Ray Loriga confirmed that I would be on the show too. She had to say that she didn't see much sense in a televised encounter, though, since the question remained: what was there for us to talk about if the project hadn't begun yet?

On the 6th of April I showed up in Madrid and taped the show with Ray Loriga, explaining what had happened so far with Sophie. Not much had occurred, but I knew how to find water where there was no fountain to speak of. Sophie never showed up at the studio. She missed the appointment in Madrid, alleging a mix-up over the date and time, and Loriga decided to turn her into the program's invited ghost. When I got back to Barcelona, in an attempt to hold my frustration in check, I sent Sophie a picture of a clock with a Portuguese caption: CONTAGEM DECRESENTE.

The message was meant as a moderately furious protest and even the seedling of a rupture, expressing that the

clock of my patience had entered countdown mode. Sophie answered immediately. She explained that she was
preparing a *wall novel* on the subject of "the missing" for
the Venice Biennale, and would be traveling the next day
to the south of France, where she would spend a stretch of
time with Florence Aubenas, the renowned "missing person" who had disappeared in another era in Iraq. She bid
adieu for a few weeks and asked me to remember that we
could take up our project again in May 2007.

It seemed to me that while in the beginning it was I who
played the part of the ghost, things had taken an unfore-
seen turn of events, and now the ghost—in Rita Malú's
story—was she. Surely, I said to myself, the spirit of the
red house on the hill on Pico Island had done a good thing
by closing the door on her *softly*.

10

I traveled to Buenos Aires at the beginning of May, ostensibly to promote my novels, but more than anything else just to disappear for a few days. I ended up hospitalized in Barcelona's Vall d'Hebron clinic when I got back. No longer did I feel the urge to go missing in an Argentine hotel room. The peculiar thing is that in Buenos Aires, I boasted about building my strength in the hotel room in Recoleta, of not setting foot at all in the streets of the city, except for the two hours I spent in a public appearance at the Book Fair. The audience smiled when I said that I had turned into a shadow, and how, like the character in one of my books, I hadn't stirred from the hotel since arriving in the city. But speaking in the style of *Journey Around My Room* was really no more than the desire to cover up a private secret: just walking down the hall was enough to make me fatigued. That was the only reason why I hadn't gone to see Recoleta Square, for example, which I remembered from previous visits. It was only two hundred meters from my hotel.

I wasn't yet aware of the worst part: I was experiencing severe kidney failure and heading toward an irreversible coma. But how could I possibly imagine something like that? How could I know that I was dying? Days went by before I fully realized what was happening. I returned to Barcelona and walked through El Prat airport like a somnambulist (a poisonous current of uric acid was reaching my brain and I didn't notice it). I answered bizarrely when they asked why I didn't have a suitcase, and my eyes rolled to the whites:

"Life has no idea what kind of life it lives."

I had spent four full days holed up in that Argentine hotel room, observing a solitary, funereal landscape (almost as if it were a premonition) outside my window: I watched the tombs of the neighboring Recoleta Cemetery, full of the pantheons of some of the Argentine homeland's national heroes. Flowers lay atop Evita Peron's mausoleum. It was an obsessive, sickly, fatal view. How was that for taking a trip?!

11

I remember W. G. Sebald's obsessive view from the hospital window, which he describes in the beginning of *The Rings of Saturn*: "I can remember precisely how, upon being admitted to that room on the eighth floor, I became overwhelmed by the feeling that the Suffolk expanses I had walked the previous summer had now shrunk once and for all to a single, blind, insensate spot. Indeed, all that could be seen of the world from my bed was the colorless patch of sky framed in the window."

Sebald recounts how over the course the day, he felt overwhelmed by the desire to look out the hospital window, draped strangely enough in black netting, to make certain that reality, as he had dreaded, hadn't vanished forever. By dusk, the desire had grown so strong that he contrived a way to slide over the edge of the bed to the floor, half on his belly and half sideways, crawling to the wall on all fours and raising himself up despite the pain. He strained to hold himself upright for the first time against the windowsill. Like Gregor Samsa, or any garden-variety beetle.

Anyway, in my case it took three days to reach the blind, insensate spot of my window on the tenth floor and to contemplate, incredulous, the surprisingly lively view extending from Vall d'Hebron to the sea. So, the world is still there after all, I told myself. It seemed amazing to me, that anthill of people I observed from way up there, feverishly crossing avenues and streets: the same mad human stream that didn't alter when the young man from Kafka's "The Judgment" threw himself out the window of his paternal home.

How far away and yet how near everything was, I thought: my hotel in Recoleta, Sophie Calle, the tombs and mausoleums with their funerary flowers, Rita Malú, Eva Perón, me myself as a dangerously missing person overseas.

12

I remember how, whenever I would finally feel optimistic, I'd end up suspecting that optimism was just another form of sickness.

13

By my fourth day in the hospital, I was able to begin reading a little and I asked for a book by Sergio Pitol. I remembered there was a shocking sentence in it that had always caught my attention—"I adore hospitals"—and I couldn't recall what came afterwards. What Pitol wrote couldn't have been closer to my own experience: "I adore hospitals. They bring back the security of childhood: all nourishment is brought to my bedside punctually. All I have to do is push a button and a nurse appears, sometimes even a doctor! They give me a pill and the pain disappears, they give me an injection, and I fall asleep on the spot ..."

Nighttime was the most difficult part of all. Pain became more of a blind, insensate spot than my window became a spot of life and the sea. I remember spending time the last night there, exploring the word *hospitality*. It seemed as good a way as any other to scare the anxiety away and forget I was in a hospital. Luckily, there was a male nurse from Guinea on the night shift, who caught my pensive mood and came to my aid, asking what was on my mind, hoping to calm my disquiet. I told him I was meditating on the word *hospitality*. First he fell quiet, but then he broke his silence, telling me never to forget that everything was relative. For example, the French had a great reputation for being hospitable people, and yet nobody dared go inside their homes. That made me laugh, and I felt at ease for the rest of the night. But come sunrise, when the first rose-tinged light entered that blind and insensate spot of my window at Vall d'Hebron, the anxiety came back with remarkable strength, and once again I coveted some movement in the air, just one, a single wisp of it: anything that would prove that I was still alive and waiting.

14

As I wait for the operation scheduled in a few weeks' time that is going to fix all my problems, I have to wear an uncomfortable medical device, which hampers my ability to move around: a catheter in my penis. I can go outside if I want to; the catheter empties into a little bag where the urine gathers. It's tied discreetly around my right leg, under my trousers. It's well hidden, but for the time being, the only thing I do outside is take a cab to the medical center on Aribau Street for tests, or to the hospital to see the nephrologist or urologist who are caring for me, or sit on the terrace of the café on the corner. Even though the doctor said I'm able to lead a normal life, I only go out when it's strictly necessary, and then I never stray very far from home.

15

I read in a note on the Internet that "the third section of Sophie Calle's *Double Game* arose from the invitation she extended to Paul Auster: to become the *author* of her acts, to invent a fictional character that she would try to resemble; she would try to live out whatever he wanted her to, for a period of one year maximum." Apparently, Paul Auster didn't want to take responsibility for what could happen to Sophie, so in exchange, he sent her a few *Personal Instructions for S. C. on How to Improve Life in New York City (Because She Asked …)*. Sophie followed his instructions, and the result was a project titled *Gotham Handbook*. The rules of the game were: smile at all times, talk to strangers, distribute sandwiches and cigarettes to the homeless, and cultivate a spot of your choice. It lasted for one week in the month of September, in 1994, and the epicenter was a phone booth located on the corner of Greenwich and Harrison. According to Sophie Calle, the result of the operation was as follows: 72 smiles received for 125 given, 22 sandwiches accepted and 10 rejected, 8 packs of cigarettes accepted and 0 rejected, 154 minutes of conversation.

I read it all, and it felt as if years had gone by since I got excited about Sophie's proposition. My physical collapse had put my health before everything else, and the concerns of our project had been relegated to sixth or seventh place in my life. So much so that Sophie Calle—her first and last names—had become dissociated from what I jotted down daily in my red notebook (I'd been making things up a lot since December).

Every so often, of course, the memory of that note I had read on the Internet returned, and brought to mind the title Paul Auster had given his work, especially the part in parenthesis, *Because She Asked*. I wasn't sure why, but I would reminisce about Sophie Calle at the most idiotic moments, and muse obsessively over the phrase, *Because She Asked*.

Whenever that happened, I couldn't help but go over everything that had ensued with Sophie, and confirm to myself once again that the ghost of the house on Pico Island had done very well to close the door *softly* on Rita Malú.

My catheter seems bent on personifying, as is happening as we speak, one of those sneering Harlequins that interrupt the drama developing on stage and untangle the plot.

In fact, the only thing the catheter, the illness, the collapse—whatever you want to call it—did, is doing, is disentangle the plot of my story with Sophie and carry me, softly, ever farther away from her.

III. THE CENTER OF THE TANGLE

1

I thought about a friend yesterday, who said that at some point we all ask ourselves what might have happened had we approached that woman in a different way, if we'd made some move or other that we hadn't. I recalled something else he said, too: "We think of our past life as if it were a sort of rough draft, something that can be transformed."

Maybe that's a good technique for escaping my life in this prison cell of my catheter. Yesterday, I went through my diary entries of the past few months, all the notes I'd been jotting down in my red notebook since last September. They serve as stimulus for reenacting the tale of my relationship with Sophie Calle in my computer. Since she hasn't made up her mind yet in this story whether or not to live out what I wrote for her in "The Journey of Rita Malú," I thought I might as well make the jump from literature to my life myself, particularly since the only thing tying me to her now, or to life, is a catheter. So I suggested to myself that I choose a few fragments from my red notebook and, following Petronius (who dared to live out what he had written), carry a few episodes over into real life, or better said, relive them and correct them if need be. As if certain notes written in my diary up to now had merely been the rough drafts of my own life.

2

I go over the first lines that I jotted down last year in my red notebook, on the 1st of September: "The sun is rising in the tall windows of my room as I initiate my red notebook or diary in which I'll write about Barcelona and other nervous cities, asking myself my name, who it is that's writing these words, and it occurs to me that my study is like a skull from which I spring anew, like an imagined citizen …"

How the hell can I ever bring to life such deeply literary sentences? I'm in the same study where I wrote them down the first time, but now I find it very difficult to feel as though my study were like a skull from which I can spring anew, like an imagined citizen.

I realize that these sentences inaugurating my diary can't possibly be translated into real life, they're pure literature. Can I seriously take a leisurely saunter around my study and pretend I'm moving around the inside of a skull? The thought makes me yawn; I mope, and feel more paralyzed than ever. Then suddenly it dawns on me that by yawning, by opening up my mouth, I've found the best way of feeling these literary sentences of mine as something *experienced*. That yawn worked a small miracle, causing me to expand and splinter like an abyss, to merge with the void. In my imagination, only the skull remains, which I am depositing at this exact moment on top of my writing table, like someone placing his head on his desk at work.

3

Still at home that evening, I decide to read the remaining entries in my red notebook all in one sitting and confirm my suspicion that until that December day when I registered Sophie Calle's call to my home in Barcelona, there was nothing of relevance in the trivial events of my life. Up to then, there was nothing significant in the notes, which are strictly rough drafts. Nothing worth correcting. In fact, it would be best to leave them as they were recorded, as what they are: the grey contours of my own life.

It's often said that literature carries a considerable advantage over life: one can go back and correct it. But in my case, I'm not interested in going back or correcting anything; I think it's better to leave it all be, at least till the day in question, when I recorded how Sophie Calle called me at home. The game changed after that. It marked a before and after in my diary, because that's when I started making the story up. Until then, my notes communicated things that really happened to me. But something changed that day, and I came up with the idea of pretending that Sophie Calle had called me at home to propose a mysterious project that she couldn't talk about over the phone. After a while, I began elaborating literarily on this quickly jotted, imaginary note, transferring it to the computer and creating a parallel fiction to what I continued crafting in my spirited red notebook of quick notes.

Why did I pretend that Sophie Calle telephoned me at home? And why did I make believe that she had asked me to write something for her to bring to life? Perhaps I made it all up precisely *because she didn't ask.*

Sophie Calle never telephoned me at home; that part belongs to my imagination. The same goes for the story of our agreements and disagreements, all make-believe. I guess I concocted the phone call and everything else because I was fed up with my own lethargic existence and needed to describe a more interesting life in my diary.

Now that I think about it, I have a make-believe story with Sophie and it's all written down. From now on, I can challenge myself to live it out instead of just imagining it. But how can I bring it to life? First of all, how can I get Sophie Calle, whom I don't know, to call me at home? It would be even more difficult to get her to meet me at Café de Flore to ask me for all these things: like proposing what she had already proposed to Paul Auster eight years ago. It's a tricky story to bring successfully to life, but nothing's impossible, and I don't want to feel defeated even before I get started. I'll take the necessary steps toward bringing the story with Sophie Calle to life, which I've been contriving and writing down. In other words, if *Don Quixote* is about a dreamer who dares to become his own dream, my story would be that of the writer who dares to bring what he has written to life, specifically, in this case, what he's invented about his relationship with Sophie Calle, his favorite "narrative artist."

4

Actually, it wouldn't be all that difficult to get Sophie to call me at home. All I need to do is talk to Ray Loriga. He was responsible for describing to me everything that Sophie had been going through over the past few months. It was he who told me about the slow agony of her mother and the funeral in Montparnasse, the details of the Venica Biennale and her friendship with Florence Aubenas. Ray explained so many particulars about Sophie, that I was able to contrive this little comedy of errors with her. Ray also told me about how, three years ago, Sophie had asked him to write a story that would allow her to bring literature to life. As Ray soon found out, she had proposed the same thing to Paul Auster, Jean Echenoz, Olivier Rolin, and very likely to other writers, too.

In fact, my make-believe relationship with Sophie began precisely on the day when Ray, a friend of hers for many years, detailed the story of Sophie's invitation for him to write her a story that she would bring to life. Ray said that everything came to a dead end, the same as what happened with Auster, Echenoz, and Rolin. I remember instantly feeling jealous when I learned about it, I would have loved for Sophie Calle to propose or ask me for something like that, especially considering all the years I've spent speculating on the relationship between life and literature, rummaging around for a technique to go beyond them, especially beyond literature.

After that, finding a way to get close to Sophie Calle became the only thing that would fetch a little joy into my life. Why shouldn't I take a stab at getting my favorite "narrative artist" to suggest bringing something that I had written to life? It seemed to me that I had as much right as anyone else to hear the proposal. Didn't I? Not only was Sophie's proposition as dangerous as it was appealing, it opened the door to a fascinating, outlandish test to push everything a step further; to go, once and for all, beyond writing itself. In fact, from a certain perspective, the challenge turned writing into a mere rag, reduced it to the condition of being a little crumb, a measly mundane procedure to gain access to life: life, which is so important. Isn't it? Isn't that what we always say? Suddenly, I felt overcome with doubt. Life, so primordial. I repeated it to myself: Life, so primordial. So essential, I added. The blood and the liver, so crucial. My doubts increased. Should life be given a place of such preference? Since the very get-go, say since Cervantes, I told myself, this tension between literature and life is what the novel has been developing all along. Truly, what we call the "novel" is nothing more than this ongoing conversation.

A few days later, I recall, I considered similar subjects on *Carta Libre*, Ray Loriga's program for Spanish television, on which I discussed my Sophie Calle story, the supposedly professional relationship I had been developing with her, as if it were true, never once letting on that it was all make-believe. Ray, who loves pretending, played along with the mischief, and Sophie became a sort of ghostly guest presence, which if you think about it, was the only way she could be on a show at all where we talked about a project that couldn't really be talked about, as I had rightly explained to Sophie in the fictional account: "What are we going to talk about on camera if the project hasn't begun yet?"

5

Waking up, I switched the briefcase-bag where the nocturnal urine gathers while I sleep (a torment) for the smaller plastic sack tied around my right leg by day. I showered and wrote down the simple dream I had that night about a woman who never turned the faucets off completely and who always closed doors very *softly*. I followed her around, doddering with my catheter and a whip, which was actually the shadow of the catheter, and my dream within a dream revealed an unprecedented image of myself: I was smacking her in the ass with that shadow.

Afterwards, I called Ray Loriga and got straight to the point. I told him I wanted Sophie Calle to call me at home as soon as possible, for her to suggest that we collaborate, then tell me that she couldn't explain it over the phone, that we should find a city, a place to meet. He giggled. I'm serious, I told him. I would appreciate that he get it done sooner rather than later, I said. Sophie had to set a date to meet in Paris, at the Café de Flore, to talk about our secret project. I myself wanted to bring to life our make-believe story that I'd been writing on my computer about our relationship. The story demanded that there be a scene in this specific café in Paris,

75

where I would like Sophie, even if she was faking it, to ask if I would write a story that she could bring to life.

Ray was a little skeptical. He had called a few days earlier to inquire after my acute renal condition that would require surgery. "You can't be serious," he said. "Oh, completely," I responded. "You honestly want to go to Paris half fucked-up, wearing a catheter, to meet Sophie and play this game with her?" he asked, and then he laughed. There was a brief silence. "What for?" It seemed a bit zealous for me to bring up Petronius and explain how I wanted to see what would happen when you live out an adventure that you had previously written, or in other words, when you take the leap from literature to your life, and so I kept quiet. "Answer me," he insisted. "Why?" Another brief silence. I answered as best I could. "To be in Paris and, more than anything else, to spend time living what I've written, instead of just writing it." Ray wanted to know why I didn't go and do something else. "Such as?" I asked, feeling more curious than a very curious boy. He didn't think twice: "You have plenty of other ways to amuse yourself, and none of them include going to Paris with a catheter to live out what you've written." I felt bad, even suspicious that I was acting against my own interests. I had the troubling impression that my desire to reach beyond it all was actually putting obstacles in my own path. I told this to Ray. "Oh the tangled web of the world," was all he said. I can't explain it, but his words soothed me, as if for the first time in my life I had shared with another person one of the most quiet and self-evident truths.

6

Two days later, I was lying on the hard shell of my back (which is just an expression, what I mean is that I was half asleep, lying naked in bed on my back, which felt very hard due to how long I had been that way; my catheter was showing since I was home alone, and I hadn't bothered to decorously cover myself with the sheets). The telephone rang, and it was Sophie Calle.

"At last, we speak again. It's about time, don't you think?" She spoke in Spanish with a thick French accent. I saw that it was a Paris number, but it hadn't yet occurred to me that it could be Sophie Calle calling, and I asked, half alarmed, who it was on the other end of the line. "I'm Sophie, I just wanted to talk to you again, so you don't think I've abandoned our project; I'm still on but I have been very busy lately …" My legs trembled slightly, as I abandoned my beetle-on-its-back position and sat up in bed. She acted as though we were a couple making up romantically after having experienced a brief separation. It wasn't what I had asked Ray for. That it was really her on the phone, the real Sophie Calle, there was no room for doubt. I had heard (and even studied) her voice in a variety of different recordings. It was her all right.

I felt as though I should play along. "Believe me, I don't expect anything from you. I've also been very busy, it'll work out," I said. But she seemed bent on clarifying things: "Venice took up a lot of my time, but the worst was the bureaucratic paperwork after my mother passed away, which was and still is utterly exhausting. I just wanted to let you know that despite the interruptions, I still want to bring your story to life …" I let her know that everything was fine, that she shouldn't worry, and for a few minutes I had the impression that I was speaking to someone familiar, as if we had known each other for a long time. I might have ended up going into details regarding my liver and urethra problems, how I was awaiting surgery, if it hadn't been for a sudden change in her tone of voice, which turned serious, even slightly aggressive.

"You're sure everything is all right? I detect a slight hint of disappointment in your voice," she said abruptly. I kept quiet and inert; I was sitting upright in bed, naked, muddled, with sudden heart palpitations. "Huh?" I asked. "I want to make a proposition, but I can't do it over the phone. Can we meet? I'd like to know if you will be coming to Paris anytime in the next few weeks." We quickly arranged to meet on Friday, the 16th of June, which was in four days, at the Café de Flore, to stage the farce. But what if she didn't mean it as a farce, and she was treating the proposal that I write a story for her in earnest? That was my great expectation. If she proposed the same as with Auster and Loriga, I could surprise her by handing over a copy of "The Journey of Rita Malú."

I called Ray to thank him for his help but couldn't reach him. Later, through mutual friends, I found that he had been called away; it had something to do with the movie he had just filmed about Santa Teresa. He wouldn't be back for a few weeks.

I decided to ask my wife to accompany me to Paris, but she flat out refused to have anything to do with such a ludicrous scheme. First comes surgery, she said. Then, after the catheter was gone, I could spend my time talking to Sophie Calle or whatever trifles I wanted. "By the way," she asked, "what's up with you and Sophie Calle? It's one thing to admire her work or get jealous of her proposals to your pal Ray; but to risk your catheter, your life, just to see her, is another story."

I knew that her words were sensible, but I also knew that art isn't, it never has been; in fact quite the contrary: it's always been an attack against common sense, an effort to get beyond the beaten path. Not only that, my wife was clearly exaggerating, since I had all the necessary medical authorizations for air travel and I wasn't risking my life by going to Paris. Besides, the adventure of living out what I had written seemed entertaining, and nothing prevented me from returning to Barcelona in time for my appointment with the anesthesiologist in Vall d'Hebron hospital on Thursday, June 22.

"What if the hospital moves the anesthesiologist's appointment forward? They warned that could happen. What then? Huh? What? You'd postpone an emergency operation because you feel like having coffee at the Flore?"

my wife asked, beyond exasperation. I don't remember how I answered her; all I know is that I couldn't convince her to come with me.

The fact is that I boarded a plane for Paris early on the 16th of June, lonesome as a rat, and with a pang of self-reproach, bearing in mind my wife's righteous indignation. Arriving like a wounded bachelor and with a return ticket to Barcelona that same evening, I showed up half an hour early to the neighborhood of Saint-Germain where the Flore is located. To be honest, I had butterflies in my stomach, more than I had expected. Ideally, I should have gone to the Café Bonaparte first and tossed back a few shots of whisky to keep wholly faithful to the story on my computer. But drinking whisky like that would have been nearly suicidal. My kidneys couldn't process the alcohol. I'd have forced them into working overtime, and in view of my physical condition, put myself at high risk. So I strolled into the Bonaparte and asked for a glass of sparkling water at the bar. I swigged it back in a single shot and asked for another. I shot that one back, too. I looked around to see if my zeal toward the fizzy water had attracted any customer's attention, but, understandably, the world remained unmoved, continuing its course without a care, without anyone wondering why I did or didn't drink those glasses of water. I went to the restroom and emptied the urine from the little plastic bag tied to my right leg. I returned to the bar, paid, and left the Bonaparte at a leisurely stride, since I still had twenty minutes before the clock struck twelve noon. I stopped at the window of La Hune bookstore, ten meters away from the Flore, and looked around to see if anyone was following me, but nobody was there. I didn't want to seem paranoid, so I stopped looking around. But, how silly of me. Who would think I was being paranoid if nobody, not a single person, was watching me?

I turned to glance in La Hune's window and saw that the books of the writer I most despise in the world were on display. Luckily, they shared space with a magnificent, sizeable reproduction of *The Bride Stripped Bare by Her Bachelors, Even*, the enigmatic double-glass piece by Marcel Duchamp that was painted in oil and divided horizontally into two equal parts with lead wire. At the top of the upper rectangle (the "Bride's Domain"), I could see the perfectly reproduced gray cloud that was painted by Duchamp. I've always heard it's the Milky Way. The cloud envelops three unpainted squares of glass, whose function (I've always heard) is to transmit to "the Bachelors" located at the bottom half of the glass the Bride's concerns, possibly her orders, her commands. I paid particular attention to what most fascinated and captivated me about this Duchampian glass: those dots peppered around the far right section of the upper panel. Those dots have always been known as the bachelor's gunshots.

I had nearly reached a point of ecstasy while contemplating the dots, but my vision betrayed me, and the books by the insufferable writer came back into sight. I considered sending him a bachelor's shot. Was I to entertain the likelihood that Sophie Calle had put those books there just to irritate me? It was highly improbable. Then I thought of the surgery waiting for me when I got back to Barcelona, and of death, and I don't know why, but I also thought that I could lose everything.

Death led me to reflecting on life. But what life? It was high time, I told myself, that in the chaos of our days, we start asking ourselves what we really mean by *life*; what exactly are we talking about when we talk about it? Maybe what we're always talking about is actually death, after all. Surely we should start trying to qualify the word *experience* … I, too, have a somewhat distant, rather fuzzy memory of it. Who lives in complete fulfillment? Is anyone truly alive? And come to think of it, what kind of life does life itself live?

I decided to exit the twilight zone into which I'd stumbled and begin speculating on what Sophie might say when we finally saw each other. That's what really mattered just then. Would she ask me to write a story for her to live, and was I to understand her proposal in the code of farce, as a mere theatrical representation? Or might she be taking it all seriously, and so when she suggested that I bring my writing beyond writing itself, I should hand her a copy of "The Journey of Rita Malú," whose twelve pages I had folded and placed so carefully in my suit pocket?

As I played it all over in my mind, I realized that I had stopped contemplating the books in the window, or paying attention to what was going on around me, and felt enveloped by a floating cloud. I was slightly startled when someone stepped between the window and me, greet-

ing me in French with a heavy Spanish accent and out-
stretched hand, politely asking what I was doing there.
I'd never seen this young person in my life, with his dark
glasses, black suit and tie, and carefully groomed four-day
beard. My offbeat sense of humor suddenly came out, and I
asked if he was the window decorator. "Because if you are, I
have some serious complaints," I said, letting a little giggle
erupt, which made me realize I wasn't all there. I had been
trying to concentrate on my meeting with Sophie Calle,
but all these obstacles were getting in my way, from my
negative thinking to this guy wearing dark glasses.

"You've been following me since the Bonaparte?" I asked
to say something, since he was just standing there, completely still, with a strange expression on his face, star-
ing at the little bulge on the inside of my right leg where
the small bag of urine was. "Don't you recognize me?"
he asked, peeking again at the tiny protuberance. I swal-
lowed hard. Could it be a drunkard, instead of that "anonymous alcoholic" I'd made up in my story based on my red
notebook? "Honestly, you don't remember me?" he asked
again. But suddenly it came to me, I recognized him. The
dark glasses had thrown me off a minute. He was a Span-
iard who'd been living in the area of Paris for a while, more
or less since I started coming back here. He liked to walk
around the district, greeting people and politely asking if
they remembered him. As long as you said yes, of course I
remember you, then he'd leave you alone. But since I had
a few minutes to kill before going to the Flore, I decided to

respond saying of course I remembered him, but that I forgot what it was he did for a living. He got very serious, pretending to be embarrassed by the question, but clearly the opposite was true, he was delighted to have the chance to respond. He took a deep breath, gratified, and said: "I'm a retired artist and now I wander the world." Oh perfect, a retired artist. No one had ever portrayed himself to me that way before. I smiled at him. He said: "I used to paint, but nobody seemed to care about what I did. So I got fed up one day and asked myself why I painted, and more importantly, why did it matter to me if anyone cared? So, guess what I did. I retired. And then I went on painting, as if nothing had happened, but only in my imagination. Take this window, for example. To me it's a still life. There's a dead crow in it. I don't think you can see it. There are days when nothing exists outside the world of my imagination. I give you my word as a retired artist."

His words had far surpassed anything I had expected to hear. But now it was time to get rid of the guy. Sophie Calle took precedence. The retired artist must retire from my sight. "Fine, see you around, I'll always remember you," I said. And I slipped away with a lively step, my body slightly inclined and head askew, as if a blustery wind were whooshing me from one side of the Boulevard Saint-Germain to the other, the catheter wild and cavorting from side to side, as I took lengthy strides forward, my hands gripping each other behind my back.

7

I entered the Flore five minutes early, but Sophie Calle was already there, and she had gotten a good table. I approached her, trying to control my small panic.

"It's me," I said with a level of shyness that was out of this world.

As a grand gesture of respect, I asked permission to be seated, and she assented and then smiled at me. I tried to conceal how difficult it was for me to sit down with the catheter. But trying to hide it only made it worse; the clumsy movement jerked my penis, and the pain lasted almost a whole minute. Unaware of my private drama, she told me we would speak in Spanish, as we had done by telephone, since she had spent a year in Mexico and could speak the language well. I curbed my shyness and anxiety by speaking up straightaway. I got started with the apparent espionage and pursuit story that I'd been subjected to just a moment earlier by an anonymous alcoholic, who seemed straight out of the *wall novels* she was so addicted to: the man and the chase, that is. She wouldn't have been the person who hired him to do it?

Sophie smiled faintly. She caressed the video camera perched atop the table and got straight to the point, no further ado. I tried to change my position to accommodate my genital equipment and catheter. But I wasn't able to improve anything. What she wanted to propose, she said, was that I write a story. That I create a character she could bring to life: one whose behavior, for one year, maximum, would be contingent on what I wrote. She wanted to change her life, she was tired of having to determine her own *deeds*, she preferred that someone else do it for her now; she wanted to let somebody else decide how she was supposed to live.

"In short," she said, "you write a story and I'll bring it to life."

We remained silent for a few slow seconds, till she went on to explain that she'd already made the same proposition to Paul Auster some years earlier, but he'd considered it too great a responsibility and declined. She had also proposed the same thing, without any luck, to Jean Echenoz, Olivier Rolin, my friend Ray Loriga, and Maurice Forest-Meyer.

"Who's that last person?" I asked distrustfully and almost unintelligibly; my question was like a humble bullet shooting underwater in a lake, like a ridiculous Bachelor's shot. But Sophie contended that now was not the time for this question. She refused to clarify who this Maurice Forest-Meyer somebody was, whose name she uttered with a trace of meaning. I realized, moreover, that what I wanted to know was something else, completely different. What

I truly wanted to extract from her was whether this was a simple mise-en-scène, or if she was being serious. But why bother asking? Whatever the response, it wouldn't serve to clarify the situation or orient me in any way. It was a useless question. So I fired another shot, this time with passion: I asked if what she really wanted was to turn me into a retired artist. The initial stupor of her look grew into what seemed to me an ice-cold glare.

I broke a lengthy silence by saying that someone had once alleged that the commanding intelligence of our species—the rich and yet vulnerable result of evolution—finds itself at times before doors that are better left unopened, or that should be closed very *softly*. Another glacial stare, which, in this specific instance, was accompanied by a look of utter bafflement. I couldn't stand it any longer, so I just blurted it out, straight from the gut, articulating every word carefully: "I am not particularly interested in reaching beyond literature."

Did she hear what I said?

"Just in case," I added, "let me say it another way. I don't want to jump any deeper into the abyss, I mean, into what lies beyond literature. There's no life there, only the risk of death. It's like these medical breakthroughs we're starting to see and that I think are really ambushes for human beings. That's why I've mentioned that there are some doors better left unopened."

"I won't deny," I continued saying, "that I've been tempted to go beyond what I've written. But on second thought, I prefer to stay where I am." No, not another step further into the abyss, the void, and no moving from literature to life. I told her I no longer wanted to abandon my writing to the whim of that sinister hole we call life. I'd been researching, exploring the shadowy abyss I intuited in the uncertain beyond of my writing, and figured it was about time to ask ourselves, especially because of the moment we were living, what were we really talking about when we talked about "life?"

Sophie said that she had to think everything over, camouflaging what seemed like a smirk. I decided to conclude, though, to finish what I had expounded, and let her know that literature would always be more interesting than this famous thing called life. First, it was more elegant, and second, I'd always found it a more powerful experience.

It's not that I was very sure of what I was saying. What was elegant was what I had said, and life would always be life, I was pretty sure of that much … No, I wasn't so sure of what I had just said so confidently. Literature is potent, and life isn't something just following in its wake.

I wasn't at all sure of what I'd just said, but it was already out there. My behavior had to do with the fact that deep down, I was annoyed because Sophie had never sincerely asked me for a story to live out on her own initiative. But why should she have? Who did I think I was? Wasn't I a mere ghost?

A song popped into my head, given Sophie's renewed and awkward silence, that went, "Love stories usually end badly." I looked Sophie straight in the eye, and it dawned on me that without realizing it, she had the ghost of Pico Island sitting in front of her. All she had to do was film me for a few seconds with her video camera, and "The Journey of Rita Malú," the story I held so carefully folded in my pocket, would come to an end right then and there.

"Anyway, I'm gone," I said.

And I took off. Outside on the street, I ran into that famous thing called life and a traffic jam that went on forever. And I crossed the street to the other side, to the other side of the boulevard.